Mermaid Reef

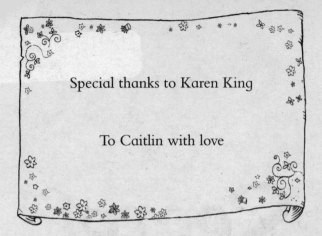

Special thanks to Karen King

To Caitlin with love

ISBN 978-0-545-53556-4

12 11 10 9 8 7 6 5 4 3 2   14 15 16 17 18 19/0

Printed in the U.S.A.   40
First Scholastic printing, May 2014

Secret Kingdom

Mermaid Reef

ROSIE BANKS

Scholastic Inc.

Contents

A Message
at School

"I'm starving!" Jasmine Smith cried as she joined her friends Ellie Macdonald and Summer Hammond at their usual table in the busy school cafeteria.

"We saved you a space." Summer smiled. "Where have you been?"

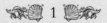

"I left my headband in the classroom," Jasmine told her. Everyone had to wear the same navy-blue sweater, white top, and boring gray trousers or skirt at school, but that didn't stop Jasmine from trying to brighten her uniform up a bit. She usually wore colorful barrettes or a pretty clip in her long dark hair. Today she was wearing a bright pink headband that matched her backpack.

As Jasmine pulled her lunchbox out of her bag, she noticed something else. Deep at the bottom of her backpack there was a familiar sparkly glow. . . .

"The Magic Box!" Jasmine whispered.

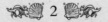

"What?" Ellie gasped, almost knocking over her drink in excitement. The Magic Box had never sent them a message at school before!

The box looked just like a beautiful wooden jewelery box. It had a curved lid with a mirror surrounded by six shiny jewels, and its sides were covered with carvings of fairies and other magical creatures. The three friends took turns taking care of it, but it really belonged to King Merry, the ruler of a wonderful place called the Secret Kingdom.

The Secret Kingdom was a magical land full of unicorns, mermaids, pixies, and elves — but it had a terrible problem. When King Merry was chosen by his subjects to rule the kingdom instead of his nasty sister, Queen Malice, the horrid

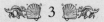

queen became so angry that she struck
six enchanted thunderbolts into the most
wonderful places in the land to ruin them
and make everyone as miserable as she.

King Merry sent the Magic Box to find
the only people who could help save the
kingdom — Jasmine, Summer, and Ellie!
The girls had already helped the king
and his pixie assistant, Trixibelle, destroy
three of the horrible thunderbolts. Now
it looked like they were needed to find
another one.

"We'll have to finish lunch when we
come back," said Ellie as they rushed into
the girls' room. Time always stood still
while they were in the Secret Kingdom,
so no one would realize they were gone.
But people might notice if they suddenly
vanished in the middle of the cafeteria!

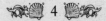

They closed the door of a stall and crowded around the box.

"The riddle's appearing!" Summer whispered.

They all watched eagerly as words started to form in the mirrored lid:

"Another thunderbolt is near,
Way down deep in water clear.
Look on the bed that's in the sea,
Where more than fish swim happily!"

Ellie slowly read out the rhyme. "What do you think that means?"

Jasmine frowned. "Well, the bottom of the sea is called the sea*bed*. . . ."

Suddenly the Magic Box glowed again and the lid magically opened, revealing the six little wooden compartments

inside. Three of the spaces were already filled with the wonderful gifts they'd been given by the people of the Secret Kingdom. There was a magical moving map that showed them all the places in the kingdom, a tiny silver unicorn horn that let them talk to animals, and a

shimmering crystal that had the power to change the weather.

"Maybe the map will give us a clue," said Jasmine. She carefully took it out of the Magic Box and smoothed it flat. It showed the whole of the Secret Kingdom spread out beneath them, as if the girls were looking down at it from high above.

"Look," Jasmine said, pointing to the aquamarine sea. Waves were gently spilling onto the shore, colorful fish were playing in the water, and a beautiful girl was sitting on a rock, combing her hair.

As Ellie, Summer, and Jasmine watched, the girl dived off the rock into the sparkling water. Jasmine gasped as she saw that, instead of legs, the girl had a glittering tail!

"Did you see that?" she cried to the

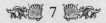

others, who nodded excitedly. "She's
a mermaid!"

Summer's eyes widened. "That must be
it! 'More than fish swim happily' — we
must be going to help mermaids!"

They leaned over the map again and
watched the mermaid as she swam
down to where an underwater town
was marked. Ellie held the map up and
looked at the place name. "'Mermaid
Reef,'" she read. "That must be where
we're going."

Jasmine and Summer agreed,
and the three friends quickly placed
their fingertips on the jewels on the
Magic Box.

Summer smiled at the others and said
the answer to the riddle out loud:
"Mermaid Reef."

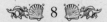

The green jewels sparkled and a glittering light beamed out from the mirror, throwing dancing patterns onto the walls. Then there was a golden flash and Trixi appeared, twirling in midair like a ballerina! Her blond hair was even messier than usual, but she had a huge grin and her blue eyes twinkled happily as she balanced on her leaf.

"Hi, Trixi," Ellie cried in delight as the pixie hovered gracefully just in front of the girls.

"Hello," Trixi said, smiling. "Goodness, where are we?"

"We're at school!" Jasmine told her.

"Oh," Trixi said as she flew around the bathroom stall on her little leaf. "This isn't at all what I thought an Other Realm school would look like. Where do you all sit?"

The girls giggled. "This isn't a classroom," Summer explained. "It's just the bathroom. We had to make sure no one would see us being swept off to the Secret Kingdom."

"Of course, silly me." Trixi smiled, but then her face took on a worried expression. "Do you know where Queen Malice's next thunderbolt is?"

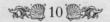

"We think so," Ellie told her. "It seems to be somewhere called Mermaid Reef."

"Then we must go at once!" Trixi exclaimed. "The mermaids will need our help."

"We *are* going to meet mermaids!" Summer squealed as she jumped up and down in excitement.

Trixi giggled, then tapped her ring and chanted:

> *"The evil queen has trouble planned.*
> *Brave helpers fly to save our land!"*

As she spoke those words, a magical whirlwind surrounded the girls, twisting and turning around them.

"Wheeee!" Summer shouted as the wind whipped her long blond hair

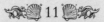

around her face.
"We're off on
another
adventure!"
Seconds
later, the
whirlwind set
them down
on a smooth
green rock in
the middle of the
aquamarine sea.
The girls were all
delighted to be wearing their sparkly
tiaras once again, although they were
still in their school uniforms!

Jasmine looked around in surprise. "I
thought we were going underwater?" she
asked Trixi, a confused look on her face.

"We are!" Trixi said with a smile as she landed on the rock beside them, rolled up her flying leaf, and tucked it under her flower hat.

Suddenly the ground beneath them started to shake.

"What's going on?" Ellie cried.

The girls watched nervously as the water began to churn in front of them, foaming and frothing as something large and dark rose up out of the depths.

A huge green head appeared out of the water. Ellie and Jasmine gasped in fear and squeezed their eyes shut, but Summer broke out in a grin. "Look!" she cried, pointing at the animal's face. The creature blinked at them with sparkling brown eyes and gave them a lazy smile. "This isn't a rock we're

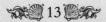

standing on — it's the back of a gigantic
sea turtle!"

"A lift from a friendly turtle is the
only way to get to Mermaid Reef!"
Trixi said. The little pixie tapped her
ring and a stream of purple bubbles shot
out of it, flying all around the girls in a
whirlwind, then bursting over their heads
and showering them with purple glitter.

"Hold on tight!" Trixi called, pointing
to the top of the turtle's shell, where
there was a ridge they could grab on to.
"One . . . two . . ."

"Trixi, wait!" Jasmine cried. "We can't
breathe underwater!"

But it was too late.

"Three!" Trixi called, tapping her ring
once more, and with a great lurch the
huge turtle dived deep into the sea. . . .

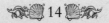

Under the Sea

Jasmine gasped in panic as the water covered her face. She quickly clamped her mouth shut tight and held her breath. "Mm-mmm!" she managed to say, waving a hand at Trixi, who was holding on to the very edge of the turtle's shell so that she would be carried along beside the girls.

Trixi gave a tinkly laugh. "Don't worry!" she explained. "That bubble dust I sprinkled you with was magical. It lets you breathe underwater. Try it!"

The turtle turned his head and gave them a big smile. Summer and Ellie let their breath go and grinned as they found that they could breathe easily. They looked excitedly at the world around them as the turtle moved smoothly through the water.

"This is amazing!" exclaimed Ellie as they whizzed past a blue jellyfish, its tentacles wriggling in the water to wave at her.

Summer laughed as the words came out of her friend's mouth in tiny bubbles, but Jasmine didn't even smile. She still had her mouth clamped shut, and her cheeks were puffed out with the effort of holding her breath.

"Jasmine, look!" Summer grinned and pointed as a school of dolphins passed by.

Jasmine's eyes sparkled as she watched the dolphins swim, but she kept her mouth tightly closed.

"It's okay," Summer said to her reassuringly. "Anyway, you're still breathing through your nose."

Jasmine let out her breath in a big bubble and laughed. "I forgot about that!"

"You looked just like a puffer fish," Ellie teased.

They held on tight as the turtle swam deeper and deeper. Soon they could see a beautiful underwater town on the sandy seabed in front of them. Tiny houses with delicate coral spires and pearly shell roofs peeped out from between the seaweed and rocks. All around the city was a beautiful coral reef, and at the top of the reef rose the turrets of a castle.

The turtle turned sharply, and pointed down with his fin.

"That must be Mermaid Reef," Ellie said.

The turtle nodded his large head and came to a smooth stop.

"We'll have to swim the rest of the way," Trixi called.

"Thanks for the lift!" Summer said as the girls hopped off the turtle's great green shell.

The turtle waved a fin and turned to swim back up to the surface.

"Wheeee!" Ellie giggled as she bobbed about, floating up a little, then flapping her arms to bring herself down again. "This is fun!"

Jasmine sank to the bottom and kicked

up some sand playfully. "It feels just like being on the beach," she said.

Trixi and the girls swam happily toward the town, chasing one another around the sea plants and rocks. Summer squealed when she noticed a tiny pink seahorse bobbing in the seaweed, its delicate tail curled around a long stem.

"Summer's made an animal friend already!" Ellie teased as she swam over. She knew Summer loved all kinds of creatures, and she and Jasmine were used to Summer wandering off and petting every cat, dog, goat, and rabbit she came

across. But Summer had never made friends with a seahorse before!

"Oh, she's adorable!" Jasmine said as the seahorse floated by. "But I don't think she's used to seeing humans at the bottom of the sea."

"She's so pretty," Summer said, reaching out to stroke the tiny seahorse's head.

"Me?" the little seahorse asked, blushing a deeper shade of pink.

Summer gasped in delight. The seahorse could understand her, and she wasn't even holding the magical unicorn horn!

"It's the bubble dust," Trixi explained with a smile. "Its magic allows you to enjoy all underwater life."

"Hello," Summer said gently. "I'm Summer, and this is Jasmine, Ellie, and Trixi."

"I'm Rosie," said the pink seahorse, her fins rippling in the current.

"Have you noticed anything strange around here, Rosie?" asked Trixi. "We think that one of Queen Malice's thunderbolts might be hidden in Mermaid Reef. It could cause a lot of trouble."

"Oh no!" Rosie gasped, ducking down to hide in the seaweed. "The whole ocean's been talking about the wicked things Queen Malice has been doing."

Ellie peered down into the weeds. "Don't worry," she told Rosie. "We won't let anything bad happen — but we have to get to the city and find that thunderbolt."

"Then I'll show you the quickest way there," the little seahorse said.

The girls followed Rosie through the
reef, and they soon arrived at a coral
gateway that led to the underwater
town. As they approached, delicate
water chimes rang out, and suddenly a
giant tentacle with rows of suckers on it
appeared over the arch!

The girls stared as an enormous
octopus climbed over the top of the arch,
glaring at them with big, beady eyes.

Ellie jumped in fright, but the octopus just lifted a tentacle and waved them through. Then it clambered back over the gate to sit next to a huge pink pearl that was resting in a giant oyster shell at the top of the entrance.

"That's the biggest pearl I've ever seen!" Jasmine giggled, turning over to swim on her back as they floated under the gateway. "Is the octopus guarding it?"

"Yes, that's the wishing pearl," explained Rosie as they swam along. "It's the most precious object in the entire ocean. Its magic is very powerful, and it can grant any wish you make."

"Wow!" Jasmine cried. "I'd love to have a wish come true!"

"Meeting a real-life mermaid will be like a wish coming true." Ellie sighed as

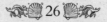

they swam farther into the town, where little shell houses were hidden among the vibrant plants and colorful seaweed. "I thought we'd have seen some by now!"

"Mermaids can make themselves invisible," Trixi told her. "So they may be around — you just might not be able to see them!"

"Does that mean there might be mermaids in our world, too?" Jasmine asked excitedly.

"Maybe," Trixi replied with a little smile. The girls looked at one another in amazement.

"Most of the merpeople will be at Coral Castle today," Rosie told them. "It's just up ahead." She pointed her tail up at a castle that rose out of the reef in front of them. It had tall, sculpted coral towers

and was decorated with thousands of shimmery pearls and shells.

"That's where Lady Merlana, the leader of the mermaids, lives," the little seahorse continued. "Every year she holds a singing contest called the Sound of the Sea Competition. All the merpeople will be there."

"Then what are we waiting for?" Jasmine grinned, kicking her feet to swim forward. "Let's go!"

Rosie led them through the castle's huge doors and then down a shell-lined corridor into a massive hall.

The girls gazed in wonder at the sight in front of them. The hall was full of hundreds of mermaids and mermen!

A few of the merpeople were flicking their long, brightly colored tails in time

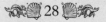

with the music. Others were dancing in
the water.

"They're beautiful!" Summer breathed.

"And there are so many of them!"
exclaimed Ellie.

Most of the merpeople were sitting and
looking up excitedly at a stage, which
was concealed by curtains of tiny shells
threaded on fine seaweed.

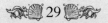

"It's the final round of the competition tonight," Rosie explained. "It's every merperson's dream to win and be known as Mermaid Reef's best singer. And the winner gets to make a wish on the wishing pearl!" she continued, glowing pinker with excitement. "They can ask for anything they want."

"I wish we could stay and watch the show." Summer sighed. "But we have to find the thunderbolt before it causes any trouble."

"Actually, I think I've found it!" Ellie cried, pointing to a black shard sticking out of the coral by one of the seats.

They all swam over to get a better look at it. Sure enough, it was the black, spiky tip of Queen Malice's thunderbolt. . . .

Lady Merlana

"Oh no!" exclaimed Jasmine. "Queen
Malice must be trying to ruin the Sound
of the Sea Competition!"

"Well, we won't let her!" Ellie
declared, putting her hands on her hips
determinedly.

"I think we had better find Lady
Merlana," said Trixi. "She needs to know
what's going on."

Rosie led Jasmine, Summer, Ellie, and

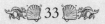

Trixi past the audience of merpeople
toward the stage. There was a ripple
of noise as the mermaids and mermen
caught sight of the girls' legs and gasped
and murmured to one another.

As they reached the stage, Trixi held
the shell curtains open for them to swim
through. "This way," she called.

They swam backstage, past lots of
dressing room doors with starfish painted
on them. One starfish sign had "Lady
Merlana" written on
it in curly writing.

Ellie knocked
on the door and it
swung open.

Inside was a
beautiful mermaid
with long, flowing

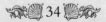

blond hair, a silver tiara, a lovely oyster-shell bikini, and a sparkling silver tail. A young mermaid with red hair was floating beside her, looking worried.

"You can do it," Lady Merlana said, comforting the mergirl. "Don't think about the audience. Just look at me and concentrate on your singing."

"I'll try, Lady Merlana," the mergirl said with a nervous smile.

As the young mermaid swam out of the door past Ellie, Summer, and Jasmine,

Lady Merlana turned and noticed them floating there. Her bright blue eyes widened with surprise. "Visitors from the Other Realm!" she gasped. "How wonderful!" She clapped her hands in delight. Just then, she noticed Trixi and Rosie swimming beside the girls and smiled. "Trixi! How lovely to see you again. Is King Merry with you? He promised to come and watch the Sound of the Sea Competition."

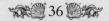

"I'm afraid not, Lady Merlana," Trixi replied. "But I'm sure he'll arrive soon." She turned to the girls. "This is Summer, Ellie, and Jasmine. They're the human girls who have been helping to stop Queen Malice's mean magic. I'm afraid we think she's going to try and wreck the Sound of the Sea Competition."

"We found one of her thunderbolts in the castle hall," added Ellie.

"Has anything gone wrong yet?" Jasmine asked.

Lady Merlana shook her head, looking confused. "No, everything's going fine. The rehearsals went well and the show is almost ready to begin."

The girls looked at one another worriedly. Queen Malice's nasty thunderbolts had always caused trouble

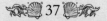

before. The horrid queen was sure to be up to something.

"Maybe we should see if the other judges have noticed anything funny," Lady Merlana suggested. "I'll give them a call." She picked up a conch shell from her dressing table and put it up to her ear.

"We use those shells to hear the sea in our world!" exclaimed Ellie as Lady Merlana murmured into the shell.

"They work even better underwater," Trixi said. "You can hear from one shell to another. The merpeople use them to talk to one another."

"Just like a telephone!" Jasmine said.

"They'll be here in a minute," Lady Merlana told them as she put the conch shell down. "I was just about to have

some sweet seaweed tea and some sea cucumber sandwiches," she continued. "Would you like some?" She pointed at a cockleshell tray laden with tiny shell cups and little triangular sandwiches.

"I'm not sure I'd like seaweed tea," Ellie whispered to Jasmine and Summer.

"Me neither," murmured Jasmine.

Summer saw Lady Merlana watching, so she politely picked up a sandwich. It was made with real sand!

"Don't worry," Rosie whispered with a giggle. "It tastes great!"

Summer took a tiny bite out of the sandwich. It was sweet and crunchy, and it tasted delicious! "Scrumptious!" She nodded, her mouth full.

"Oh, good," Jasmine cried, taking a sandwich eagerly. "I'm starving. We never had a chance to finish lunch!"

A couple of minutes later, two breathtakingly beautiful mermaids and a handsome merman arrived. The mermaids' long hair tumbled down onto their shoulders and their bikinis were made from oyster shells.

One of them had a golden tail and the other's was a shimmering lilac color. The merman had black hair, dark brown eyes, and a green tail. When he smiled he revealed a set of dazzling pearl-white teeth.

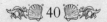

"Girls, this is Cordelia, Meredith, and Zale," Lady Merlana said as she pointed to the two mermaids and the merman. "Nice to meet you," Summer said with a smile.

"Judges, this is Summer, Jasmine, and Ellie," Lady Merlana continued, nodding at each girl in turn. "They're *humans*!" she added in a loud whisper to the judges.

"My goodness, just look at their legs!" squealed Cordelia as she swam over to meet them.

The girls all felt a bit awkward in front of such glamorous merfolk, especially when they were still in their school uniforms, but the merpeople seemed delighted to meet them.

"I've always wanted to see a real-life human!" exclaimed Meredith.

"Wonderful to meet you." Zale beamed.

Cordelia and Meredith swam forward to hug Summer and Jasmine, and Zale floated over to shake Ellie's hand.

Cordelia was very excited, and kept comparing her tail to Summer's legs, looking at her feet, and touching her shoes.

Summer giggled and shyly reached out to touch the mermaid's lilac tail. It was covered with tiny scales, just like a fish, but it was smooth and sleek. She bent down to feel one of Cordelia's big, broad fins, but suddenly there was a loud clap of thunder, and the mermaid disappeared in a cloud of bubbles!

Vanished!

"Oh no!" Summer cried. "What did I do?"

"It wasn't you," Trixi reassured her, looking around the room. "The other judges have vanished, too!"

"What's happened?" gasped Lady Merlana. "Where have they gone?"

"Have they made themselves invisible?" Jasmine asked.

Lady Merlana shook her head. "No, I'd still be able to see them if they had. They've completely disappeared!"

"I'll try to magic them back," Trixi said. She tapped her ring, but nothing happened. She shook her head sadly. "If my magic won't work, this definitely has something to do with the queen's thunderbolt."

"But the competition is due to start any minute!" Lady Merlana cried. She flicked her tail anxiously. "What am I going to do without my judges?"

Just then a line of bubbles started streaming out of the conch shell. Lady Merlana picked it up and put it against her ear. She listened for a second, then turned to the girls. "There's a funny-looking ship outside the castle," she told them. "Maybe that has something to do with Queen Malice's thunderbolt?"

"Let's go and check," Jasmine said,

swimming over to the window, which
was made of big bubbles instead of glass.

   As they peered out, they saw a blue-and-
white polka-dotted submarine moving
backward over the sand. Through the
porthole they could see a small, round
man with white hair and a long beard
sitting inside. He was peering through the
boat's periscope with a confused look on
his face.

"It's only King Merry!" Summer sighed in relief.

"Look!" Ellie grinned. "The submarine's periscope is coming out of the bottom, not the top!"

Trixi smiled. "Another of his wonky inventions," she whispered.

Trixi tapped her ring, and in a flash the periscope was the right way around and King Merry could see them all waving at him.

The submarine came to a halt, and the king swam out, his half-moon spectacles perched crookedly on his nose. He was wearing a royal-blue wet suit with a golden crown pattern on it. His real crown was balanced on top of a large, round diver's helmet that looked like an upside-down goldfish bowl.

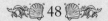

Trixi floated across to him and helped him take his helmet off, then burst some purple bubbles over him so that he could breathe.

King Merry sneezed so hard that his glasses blew off his nose and onto the sand.

Lady Merlana scooped them up

and gave them back to him. "Welcome to Mermaid Reef, Your Majesty," she said. "We're very pleased that you've come to watch the show."

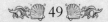

"I'm looking forward to it," King Merry replied as he put his glasses back on. "Hello, girls," he said, smiling at Ellie, Summer, and Jasmine. "Have you come to see the show, too?"

"They've come to find another one of Queen Malice's thunderbolts," said Trixi. "And there might not be a show unless we find the judges! The thunderbolt has made them disappear."

"Oh dear." King Merry sighed, looking very worried.

"Where should we start searching?" asked Ellie.

"I don't know if we should look for them—" Summer started to say, then blushed as everyone stared at her. "I mean . . . well . . . at Unicorn Valley and Cloud Island, things went back to normal

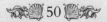

once we'd broken Queen Malice's spell," she pointed out. "And now she's trying to spoil the Sound of the Sea Competition. So if we make sure her nasty magic doesn't wreck it, then the judges should appear again."

"Hey, you're right," agreed Ellie.

"Anyway, the judges could be anywhere in the Secret Kingdom," added Jasmine. "It would take us ages to search the whole island."

Trixi nodded. "That makes sense. Queen Malice just wants to keep them out of the way so the competition will be ruined."

"But it *will* be ruined if the judges aren't here," replied Lady Merlana sadly.

"Couldn't someone else judge the acts?" asked Ellie. "What about King Merry?"

"Well . . . er . . . I'd love to help, of course," the king stammered. "But I don't think I'd be of much use. I'm tone-deaf and I don't know anything about singing!"

"But I know someone who does," suggested Trixi. "Jasmine! And Ellie makes fantastic clothes, so she can judge the costumes. And Summer is brilliant with words, so she can judge the songwriting."

The girls all stared at her with their mouths wide open.

"Us?" Summer squeaked.

"Why not?" asked Trixi. "You'd be perfect!" King Merry and Rosie nodded their heads in agreement.

"What a splendid idea," Lady Merlana said approvingly. "And just in time, as the competition is about to begin! Will you help us?"

"Of course!" the girls cried together.

Lady Merlana smiled and led them over to the stage.

"I can't believe I'm going to judge a mermaid singing competition!" Jasmine squealed.

But when they saw all the merpeople waiting for the show to begin, even Jasmine began to feel nervous.

"I'm not sure about this," Summer whispered to Ellie. "The merpeople are expecting to see three glamorous judges. What are they going to think of us in our school uniforms?"

"I can fix that," Trixi said. She tapped her ring and instantly their school uniforms were transformed into beautiful outfits. Summer had on a long yellow dress decorated with silver sequins, Jasmine

wore a sparkly
pink top with
black leggings
and silver
ankle boots,
and Ellie had
on a shimmery
emerald-green
dress with purple
swirls on it. The
jewels on their tiaras
glittered beautifully, reflecting the colors
of their outfits.

"There you go!" Trixi said, looking very
pleased with herself.

"You all look beautiful," Rosie told
them shyly.

Jasmine, Ellie, and Summer were
delighted. Now they couldn't wait for the

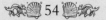

show to start! They treaded water
backstage while Trixi, Rosie, and King
Merry floated over to find their seats
among the merpeople in the audience.

Finally the shell curtains opened
and Lady Merlana swam onto the
stage. "Mermaids and mermen," she
announced. "We have some very special
guests to judge the Sound of the Sea
Competition this year, all the way from
the Other Realm."

There were gasps and cries from
the audience. Lady Merlana turned
and beckoned for the girls to join her.
"Presenting . . . Summer, Jasmine, and
Ellie!"

The girls grinned with excitement. It
was time for the contest to begin!

The Sound of the Sea

The audience murmured as the girls swam out and the curtains closed.

"They don't have tails!" one merman whispered, sounding shocked.

"People from the Other Realm have legs instead, silly," replied the mermaid sitting next to him.

Summer, Jasmine, and Ellie felt very important as the merpeople whispered and stared, some of them floating up off their seats so they could get a better look at the humans' legs.

The girls smiled and waved as they took their places in front of the stage.

As soon as they sat down, the shell-curtains opened again and Lady Merlana announced the first contestant, a golden-haired mermaid named Nerissa, who was wearing a pretty seaweed bikini dress that draped over her shiny blue tail. For a moment Nerissa hesitated nervously, and Summer felt sorry for her. She smiled encouragingly and the mermaid smiled back, then started to sing.

Nerissa sang a haunting song about a lonely old sea witch. As she sang,

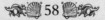

tears started to roll down her cheeks,
transforming into beautiful pearls that
floated around her. When the song ended
the pearls glowed, changing color from
white to pink to gold before disappearing
in a flash.

The audience clapped and cheered, thumping their tails down on the seabed. Summer, Jasmine, and Ellie jumped up to give Nerissa a standing ovation.

The mermaid waved and blew kisses to the audience before she swam offstage.

"That was fantastic!" exclaimed Ellie as they sat back down again. "Her costume was gorgeous!"

"She sang so beautifully it made me cry, too," sniffed Summer, wiping the tears from her eyes.

"It was an excellent performance," agreed Jasmine, who was taking her judging responsibilities very seriously.

Next, Lady Merlana announced Atlanta, a red-haired mermaid with a shimmering lilac tail and a blue seaweed top. She was joined by four white

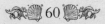

angelfish with long tails, which were tied with cute purple bows. They danced around her as she sang a soft melody about a little fish that couldn't find its way home and was finally rescued by a mermaid.

Summer loved watching the angelfish dancing in time to the gentle song, and cheered extra loudly as they bowed.

Next up was a handsome merman named Orcan, with blond hair and a dashing silver tail. He sang a soulful song that made the sea seem calmer. Halfway through the performance, the girls heard the distant sound of whale song, as if a whale was answering the merman.

The girls listened in wonder as the whale song got louder. There was a ripple of excitement around the room.

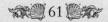

Then Jasmine turned around and
caught her breath — through the window
she could see an enormous eye!

It was a gigantic blue whale, who had
joined in with Orcan's song, turning it
into a magical duet.

"That was incredible!" Summer gasped,
clapping in delight as the gentle whale
grinned at her.

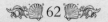

The audience was thrilled. Once again they cheered and thumped their tails down on the seabed as the merman bowed, then left the stage.

"Amazing!" declared Jasmine. "Everyone's so good I don't know how we're going to choose a winner."

Finally the last contestant, Nerin, came onto the stage. She was a tiny mermaid dressed in an enormous red silk gown that almost covered her tail completely.

To everyone's amazement, her voice was so powerful that it made the waves lash wildly above the castle. As the notes became higher and higher, the movement of the waves crashed through the water in the hall, rocking everyone from side to side.

"Ooh, I feel seasick!" gasped Ellie, clinging to her seat.

"Her voice must be very powerful to make the waves crash like that," Jasmine said admiringly.

Suddenly the sea seemed to go dark.

"That's not the singing, is it?" Jasmine whispered to Ellie, who shook her head.

Nerin's voice trailed off as the water got darker and blacker.

"Wh-what's that?" Summer asked, pointing out the bubble windows.

A dark shape was creeping into view overhead. As it got closer, the girls saw that it was a large black boat with an anchor shaped like a thunderbolt.

"It's Queen Malice's yacht!" King Merry cried in alarm.

Summer felt a chill run through her as a shadowy figure with spiky hair and batlike wings dropped out of the yacht and down into the water. Then another and another.

"Oh no!" she shouted in horror. "It's the Storm Sprites!"

The Wishing Pearl

When the merpeople saw the Storm Sprites, they all started to panic.

"I'm sure there's nothing to worry about," Lady Merlana reassured everyone. "Please stay calm and don't get your tails in a twist!"

The sprites were all wearing diving masks and snorkels, and they had flippers over their feet and hands. They swam

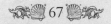

along awkwardly, their leathery wings
struggling through the water, as they
headed toward the arch at the entrance
to the reef.

"They're after the wishing pearl!"
Summer realized with a gasp.

"Don't worry, everyone," said Lady
Merlana confidently. "My octopus guard
will stop them."

Sure enough, as the Storm Sprites
approached, the octopus appeared at
the top of the gateway and wrapped its
tentacles protectively around the oyster
shell. The merpeople breathed a sigh of
relief.

But suddenly a thunderbolt burst
out from Queen Malice's yacht like a
torpedo. A loud crash echoed through the

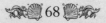

water and the octopus disappeared in a
cloud of bubbles, just like the judges had.

Lady Merlana cried out and started
swimming toward the arch, her powerful
tail propelling her along quickly. Trixi
and the girls set off behind her as King
Merry and Rosie watched in horror.

The girls swam as quickly as they
could, but their legs couldn't keep up with
Lady Merlana's fins.

"She's not going to reach the pearl in time!" Jasmine shouted to the others as they swam. "The sprites are too close to it already!"

"That pearl is very powerful," Trixi said, flying her leaf through the water frantically. "If Queen Malice gets hold of it, she'll be able to wish for all kinds of horrible things!"

Ellie stopped swimming. "We'll never catch up," she cried. "But we have to do something!"

The others gathered around and treaded water while they tried to think of what to do.

"Could you magic up a big wave to wash the sprites away?" Summer asked Trixi.

"Too dangerous," the little pixie replied. "It might wash the pearl away, too."

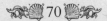

"How about trapping them?" Jasmine suggested. "Could you magic up a shell or a big bubble?"

"That might work," Trixi said excitedly.

"Quick!" shouted Ellie as the lead sprite reached out his spiky fingers for the pearl. "You have to do it now!"

Trixi tapped her ring and suddenly each sprite was surrounded by the shimmering walls of a sparkling bubble. The bubbles floated up and down in the current as the Storm Sprites shouted and banged their flippers against the walls.

"That should stop them long enough for Lady Merlana to get the pearl," Trixi said. "Come on!"

Lady Merlana swam past the bubbles, looking at the sprites inside in amazement. Then, with a flick of her tail, she floated up to the wishing pearl, which was still lying in the giant oyster shell at the top of the gateway.

"We've got to hurry!" gasped Summer, swimming up behind her. "They won't be trapped for long. We have to hide the pearl!"

"But where can we hide it?" Jasmine asked as she arrived, out of breath.

"You can't," came a voice from above them.

The girls gasped in horror as Queen Malice appeared overhead, riding on top of a gigantic black stingray. She snatched the wishing pearl from its shell.

"Ha!" Queen Malice gave a triumphant laugh. "It's mine and there's nothing you can do about it! Finally I will get what I deserve!"

As the girls watched in dismay, she held the pearl high above her head and cried, "I wish I was the ruler of the Secret Kingdom, and all my subjects obeyed me!"

Queen Malice's Wish

All at once there was a huge shudder and the water rippled around the girls. Summer, Jasmine, and Ellie grabbed one another's hands to steady themselves.

Queen Malice laughed wickedly as she put her hands up to her head to touch the pointy crown that now rested there — it was King Merry's crown!

One of the sprites took the flippers off his hands and dug his pointy fingers into the bubble that surrounded him. It burst with a loud *pop*. The others followed and, snickering, they paddled over to Queen Malice, cheering and laughing.

"Silence!" Queen Malice commanded, turning to look at Lady Merlana and Trixi. "Greet your ruler!" she demanded.

Lady Merlana bent her tail and gave
a deep bow, and Trixi flew up to Queen
Malice and curtsied to her. "How can I
serve you, Your Majesty?" the little pixie
asked in a strange, blank voice.

Summer gasped. "What's happening?"
she whispered to Jasmine and Ellie. "Why
are Trixi and Lady Merlana doing what
she says?"

"It must be the wish," Ellie said. "We
seem to be the only ones who aren't
affected."

"It's got to be because we're not from
the Secret Kingdom," Summer said. "So
we're not her subjects!"

Queen Malice turned to look at them.
Before Ellie or Summer could move,
Jasmine had dropped into a deep curtsy.

"Your Royal Highness," she said, turning her head and winking at her friends.

The Storm Sprites all sneered.

"Enough!" Queen Malice snapped. "There will be lots of time to taunt these meddling girls when they're locked in my dungeons! Now everyone follow me back to the yacht!"

"Yes, my queen," Lady Merlana and Trixi chanted, as if they were hypnotized.

"Yes, my queen," the girls repeated.

Queen Malice pulled on the reins and her stingray started swimming up toward the yacht. Ellie, Summer, and Jasmine followed along behind Trixi, Lady Merlana, and the Storm Sprites.

"Good idea, Jasmine," Ellie whispered. "Now she thinks her wish has affected us, too."

"Thanks," Jasmine said. "But we still need to find a way to stop her!"

The girls looked ahead at Queen Malice, who was cackling to herself and wishing for more and more things. They watched as she passed a jeweled coronet and a pair of diamond shoes back for the Storm Sprites to carry. Finally she passed the pearl to the sprite behind her and urged the stingray to swim faster.

"We've got to get that pearl back!" Summer said determinedly. "Before things get any worse!"

"I have an idea," Ellie said. "Follow my lead!"

The three girls kicked forward with their feet until they were swimming alongside the lead sprite.

"You're so lucky to be Queen Malice's

servant," Ellie said to the sprite enviously.
"It's such an important job."

"Yeah," Jasmine joined in. "I wish we
could do something to help her."

The sprite looked pleased. "Oh, we've
got lots of jobs that you can do!" He
laughed nastily. "You can clean out
the gnome toilets and cook the bats'
breakfast and feed the stink toads."

"Oh, thank you!" Jasmine said, acting
as though the sprite had just given her a
piece of chocolate cake. But her eyes were
fixed on the pearl, which he was holding
with his pointy fingers. It was moving up
and down as he swam, so close she could
almost touch it. . . .

"Hurry up, back there!" Queen Malice
snarled. "Can't you swim any faster?

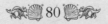

I want to go back to my castle and start causing chaos all around the kingdom!"

"Yes, Your Majesty!" the sprites chorused obediently.

"I could swim a lot faster without all of this stuff. . ." the sprite nearest to Summer grumbled under his breath as he dragged along a treasure chest that was overflowing with jewels. He looked over at Summer and a smile crossed his face. "I know! You can carry it all!" He dumped the heavy box into Summer's arms gleefully.

The other sprites laughed as they saw Summer struggling under the weight of the chest.

"Good idea!" one chuckled as he passed a silver cloak and a huge mirror to Ellie. "You can take this."

"Yeah!" said the lead sprite. "And this, too!" He passed Jasmine the wishing pearl.

Jasmine gasped at she looked down at the wishing pearl in her hands. The sprite suddenly realized his mistake and reached for the pearl, but it was too late.

"I wish all Queen Malice's wishes were undone and she was far away from here!" Jasmine shouted.

"Noooooooo!" Queen Malice screamed, trying uselessly to hold on to King Merry's crown as a vast whirlpool started

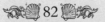

twirling around her, twisting it away from her grasping fingers.

The Storm Sprites swam over and tried to catch her and pull her out, but they were sucked into the whirlpool, too.

"You haven't won!" Queen Malice screeched as she spun farther and farther into the watery hole. "I'll get all of you! One day I will rule the kingdom. . . . Just you wait and seeeeeeee!"

All at once the whirlpool disappeared, and the girls were left floating next to Lady Merlana and Trixi, who were shaking their heads as if they were waking up from a bad dream.

Jasmine turned to Lady Merlana and handed her the wishing pearl. "I think this belongs to you." She grinned.

And the Winner Is . . .

"How can I ever thank you enough?"
Lady Merlana asked, hugging each of the
girls in turn. "You've saved us all!"

As they swam back into Mermaid Reef,
Jasmine, Ellie, and Summer could see the
rest of the merpeople gathered outside
the castle, waiting for them to return.

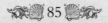

"Don't worry," Ellie shouted as they got closer. "Queen Malice and her nasty Storm Sprites are gone!"

King Merry and Rosie swam over to greet them.

"Did you lose this?" Ellie asked King Merry as she handed him his crown.

King Merry patted his head. "Oh my goodness!" he cried out. "Thank you very much."

Rosie bobbed up to Summer, who held out her little finger so that the seahorse could curl her tail around it.

"Yes, thank you," Lady Merlana said to the girls as she cradled the precious wishing pearl carefully in her arms. "You've stopped Queen Malice from using the wishing pearl to bring disaster to Mermaid Reef, and you've saved the Secret Kingdom once again."

"There's still one thing we haven't fixed, though," Ellie reminded her. "We still need to break Queen Malice's thunderbolt to get the judges back."

Lady Merlana put her hands to her mouth in surprise. "I was so relieved to have the wishing pearl back that I almost forgot!" she gasped. "We have to finish the Sound of the Sea Competition!"

"The show must go on!" Jasmine smiled.

Lady Merlana led everyone back to Coral Castle. The merpeople returned

to the audience and Jasmine, Summer, and Ellie took their places in the judges' chairs.

The girls huddled together at the table to discuss the acts. They all agreed that Nerissa, the mermaid whose tears turned to pearls, and Orcan, the merman who sang with the whale, were the best acts. But they just couldn't decide who was better.

"They both sang wonderfully, but I think Nerissa was the best performer," said Jasmine.

"I liked Orcan and the whale," Summer said shyly.

"The audience cheered just as loudly for both of them," added Ellie, thinking hard. "I know!" she declared suddenly.

She told her idea to Summer and

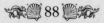

Jasmine, who both nodded happily. Then she floated over to Lady Merlana and whispered in her ear.

Lady Merlana smiled, then floated to the center of the stage. A hush fell over the audience.

"Mermaids and mermen," she started. "We've had a wonderful competition this year and all our contestants deserve a big round of applause."

The audience flapped their tails down on the sea floor and the hall filled with claps and cheers.

Eventually Lady Merlana held up her hand for silence.

Trixi, King Merry, and Rosie looked at one another excitedly as they waited for Lady Merlana to announce the winner. Which act had the girls chosen?

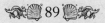

"Ellie, Summer, and Jasmine have made a decision," Lady Merlana continued, ". . . and . . . for the first time ever . . ." She stopped and everyone in the audience held their breath.

"We have a tie!" she declared. "The winners are Nerissa and Orcan."

Trixi and King Merry exchanged grins of delight. The audience cheered wildly as Lady Merlana put garlands of colorful sea anemones around the winners' necks, then presented each of them with a starfish medal.

Glowing algae lit up the sea around Nerissa and Orcan as they hugged each other and Lady Merlana, crying tears of happiness.

Suddenly there was a loud cracking sound from somewhere backstage.

"It sounds like the thunderbolt has broken!" gasped Ellie.

There was a burst of bubbles and the merperson judges appeared in front of them, looking a little dazed.

"You've broken Queen Malice's spell!" Trixi cheered.

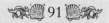

"Have we missed the competition?" Cordelia asked worriedly. Lady Merlana explained how the girls had taken their places and stopped Queen Malice from stealing the wishing pearl.

"Oh, thank you!" Cordelia cried. "You saved the day!"

"We should be thanking all of *you*!" exclaimed Ellie. "We've had such a wonderful time here that now we don't want to go home!"

"Well, there's one more thing you simply have to see," said Lady Merlana as she beckoned Nerissa and Orcan over. She turned to the singers and smiled. "It's time for you to make a wish on the pearl," she told them.

Everyone gathered around as Nerissa and Orcan floated in front of the magic pearl. They both looked very thoughtful for a moment, and then Nerissa leaned over and whispered something in Orcan's ear.

Orcan smiled and nodded. "We've decided," he said seriously.

"We'd like to give our wish to Jasmine, Ellie, and Summer," Nerissa said with a smile. "After all, if it wasn't for them, the wishing pearl would still be in Queen Malice's hands!"

Jasmine, Ellie, and Summer gasped in surprise. Nerissa and Orcan swam over to give them the pearl, and the three girls laid their hands on it.

"Whatever are we going to wish for?" Ellie asked.

"I know what I'd like," Summer said shyly. Her friends leaned in to listen to her. "I'd love to see how it feels to be a

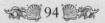

mermaid, and to have a beautiful tail of my own!"

Jasmine and Ellie grinned. What a brilliant idea!

"We wish that we could be mermaids — just for a little while," Jasmine said.

The wishing pearl glowed brightly, bathing them all in sparkly pink light.

Ellie shut her eyes, and when she opened them she saw that she had a gorgeous orangey-red tail that matched her hair! She looked over and saw that Summer now had a pretty seaweed green tail, and Jasmine had a shimmering silver one.

"We're mermaids!" Ellie cried, flicking her tail and somersaulting in excitement. "We're really mermaids!"

The girls spent the rest of the day

swimming around, chasing the other
mermaids, and playing hide-and-seek —
which was a lot harder when you could
turn invisible!

But all too soon the wish wore off and
the girls' tails turned back into legs.

"We should probably go home,"
Jasmine said reluctantly.

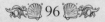

"But we've had such an amazing time!"
Summer added.

Lady Merlana hugged them all
good-bye. "I've got a gift for you as
well," she said, holding out a beautiful
silver pearl. It looked like a small version
of the wishing pearl.

"This is to say thank you," she said.
"You can use it to turn invisible, just
like merpeople do." She handed it to
Jasmine — who promptly disappeared.

"This is wonderful." Jasmine giggled
as she invisibly tickled Summer and
Ellie.

"It doesn't last for long," Lady Merlana
warned them. "So you'll have to be
careful when you use it. But hopefully
it will help you fight Queen Malice's
horrible magic."

Lady Merlana hugged each girl again and then swam back to her subjects. Trixi, Rosie, and King Merry rushed over to say good-bye, too.

"You will come back soon, won't you?" King Merry asked worriedly. "There are still two more thunderbolts hidden in the kingdom, and we'll never be able to destroy them without you."

"Of course we will," Jasmine told him. "We'll come whenever you need us."

The girls waved good-bye to their
new friends as Trixi tapped her ring and
created a whirlpool that spun around
them and transported them back to the
human world.

A few seconds later they found themselves back in the girls' room at school, as if they'd never left.

"I'd forgotten we were at school!" Ellie gasped. "How funny that we have to go to English class now, when we've spent all lunchtime swimming with mermaids!"

"Lunch isn't over yet, silly," Jasmine reminded her. "It's the same time now as when we left. Which is lucky, because I'm still hungry!"

"We'd better put our new gift away before we go and eat," said Ellie, holding out the Magic Box.

The lid on the box sprang open, and Jasmine carefully put the special pearl into one of the empty compartments.

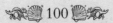

"I wonder where we'll go for our next adventure," said Summer.

"I don't care," giggled Ellie. "But I hope we go during school time again — visiting the Secret Kingdom is much more fun than being in class!"

In the next Secret Kingdom
adventure, Ellie, Summer, and
Jasmine visit

Magic Mountain

Read on for a sneak peek . . .

A Nighttime
Adventure

"I'm Queen Malice!" cried the girl in
black. She shook her long, dark hair back
from her face. "Get them, Storm Sprites!"
Two small creatures with black wings ran
into the room and cackled nastily.

Summer Hammond and Ellie Macdonald squealed and dived over the living room sofa. The girl in black was only their friend Jasmine Smith, dressed in an old sheet and waving a thunderbolt made from a painted stick. But her acting was so good that it almost seemed like nasty Queen Malice was in the room!

The Storm Sprites were Summer's little brothers, Finn and Connor, dressed up to look like Queen Malice's horrible gray-skinned, spiky-fingered helpers. Ellie had tucked old towels into their T-shirts and folded them in the shape of the Storm Sprites' batlike wings.

The boys shrieked with excitement and ran across the room to grab Summer's legs as she tried to scrunch herself up behind the sofa.

"Got you!" Connor giggled.

"That's what you think." Summer laughed, jumping up and tickling him. Ellie did the same to Finn.

"Foolish sprites!" scolded Jasmine in a dramatic voice. "Do I have to do everything myself?" She poked Summer with the thunderbolt stick.

"Connor, Finn!" Summer's stepdad called from the kitchen. "Bath time!"

Summer let Connor go and went to the door. "They're coming!" she called back. "Sorry, guys," she told her little brothers. "We have to stop playing now."

"But I want to be a Storm Sprite," said three-year-old Finn, sticking out his bottom lip.

"Storm Sprites aren't real, silly," five-year-old Connor told him scornfully.

Summer grinned at Jasmine and Ellie over her brothers' heads. Little did the boys know that Storm Sprites *were* real, and that they lived in a magical land called the Secret Kingdom!

The Secret Kingdom was a wonderful place full of pixies, unicorns, mermaids, and all kinds of magical creatures, but it was in trouble — and only Ellie, Summer, and Jasmine could help.

One day not very long ago, the girls had found a magical box at a school rummage sale that had transported King Merry, the ruler of the Secret Kingdom, and his royal pixie, Trixi, to the human world. King Merry and Trixi had asked the girls for their help in stopping Queen Malice, the king's evil sister, from causing trouble in the kingdom.

Queen Malice had been so angry when King Merry had been chosen to rule the Secret Kingdom instead of her that she had hidden six horrible thunderbolts around the land. She had cast spells on each of the thunderbolts so they would cause chaos and ruin all the fun in the kingdom.

Jasmine, Ellie, and Summer had already found four of the thunderbolts and broken their nasty spells. But until the Magic Box called them into the kingdom again, all they could do was *play* at fighting Queen Malice and the Storm Sprites!

Summer, Ellie, and Jasmine helped Finn and Connor take off their costumes, then sent them off to take a bath.

The girls headed up toward Summer's room to watch a DVD. As they passed the big window in the hall, they saw it was dark and frigid outside.

"Maybe it will snow again tonight," said Jasmine hopefully.

"Brrrr," said Ellie, pushing her wiry red curls back from her face as she looked into the gloomy garden. "Perfect weather for a sleepover!" She grinned.

They went into Summer's room, which was painted a soft yellow and had lots of animal posters all over the walls. Summer put on her comfy old yellow-flowered pajamas. Ellie got into her green-and-purple pair and then they both admired Jasmine's shorts and tank set, which were brand-new and covered with big pink polka dots.

"What shall we watch?" asked Summer, looking through her pile of DVDs.

But Jasmine and Ellie weren't paying attention. They had taken the Magic Box down from among the rows of books and piles of stuffed toys on Summer's tall bookcase and put it on top of Ellie's sleeping bag.

The Magic Box was about the size of a jewelery box and was heavy and wooden. The sides were carved with pictures of magical creatures, and it had a mirror set into its curved lid, which was surrounded by six beautiful green gemstones.

"I know what I'd like to watch," said Ellie. "The Magic Box shining!"

"Ooh, yes!" agreed Jasmine, tracing the carvings with her finger. "And a riddle appearing to tell us where the next thunderbolt is!"

Jasmine lay on her front and stared at the box, willing a message to appear, until her eyes watered. "It's no good!" she said finally. "Let's just put a movie on."

Summer put in a DVD, and the girls ended up laughing so much that Mrs. Hammond had to come in and tell them it was bedtime. After that they talked in whispers for a while, then one by one they drifted off to sleep.

In the middle of the night, Summer suddenly woke up. Blinking sleepily, she looked around to find out what had disturbed her.

Ellie and Jasmine were curled up in their sleeping bags on the floor, and everything looked normal. Then Summer realized what was strange — the fact that she could see at all! Instead of being dark, her room was lit up by a dim glow.

But it can't be morning already, she thought. Then she glanced up at her shelves and her heart jumped with excitement — the light was coming from the Magic Box!

Suddenly feeling wide-awake, she slipped out of bed and crept between the two sleeping bags that were taking up most of her floor. With trembling hands, she nudged Ellie and Jasmine.

"The Magic Box," she whispered, reaching up to get it. "It's glowing!"

Ellie and Jasmine woke up and quickly scrambled out of their sleeping bags.

As the girls gathered around the box, light flickered across their faces and

words began to form in the mirror on
its lid:

"*Where the brownies slide, not run,*
Where they ride on boards for fun,
Where cheeks are red and breath is white,
That's where you must go tonight!"

Read
Magic Mountain
to find out what
happens next!

Be in on the secret.
Collect them all!

Enjoy six sparkling adventures.
www.secretkingdombooks.com

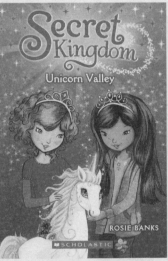

Character Profile:
Queen
Malice

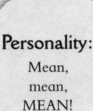

Personality:
Mean,
mean,
MEAN!

Favorite
Place in the
Secret
Kingdom:
The dingy dungeons of
Thunder Castle.

Family:

King Merry is her brother, but she'd rather play with a stink toad than with him.

Favorite Color:

Black

Loves:

Making the people of the Secret Kingdom miserable, and dreaming of the day she will be their ruler.

Spot the Difference

Jasmine, Ellie, and Summer are ready for adventure! Can you spot five differences between the two pictures?

RAINBOW magic™

Which Magical Fairies Have You Met?

- ❏ The Rainbow Fairies
- ❏ The Weather Fairies
- ❏ The Jewel Fairies
- ❏ The Pet Fairies
- ❏ The Dance Fairies
- ❏ The Music Fairies
- ❏ The Sports Fairies
- ❏ The Party Fairies
- ❏ The Ocean Fairies
- ❏ The Night Fairies
- ❏ The Magical Animal Fairies
- ❏ The Princess Fairies
- ❏ The Superstar Fairies
- ❏ The Fashion Fairies
- ❏ The Sugar & Spice Fairies
- ❏ The Earth Fairies

SCHOLASTIC

Find all of your favorite fairy friends at
scholastic.com/rainbowmagic

RMFAIRY

RAINBOW magic™

SPECIAL EDITION

3 stories in each one!

Which Magical Fairies Have You Met?

- ☐ Joy the Summer Vacation Fairy
- ☐ Holly the Christmas Fairy
- ☐ Kylie the Carnival Fairy
- ☐ Stella the Star Fairy
- ☐ Shannon the Ocean Fairy
- ☐ Trixie the Halloween Fairy
- ☐ Gabriella the Snow Kingdom Fairy
- ☐ Juliet the Valentine Fairy
- ☐ Mia the Bridesmaid Fairy
- ☐ Flora the Dress-Up Fairy
- ☐ Paige the Christmas Play Fairy
- ☐ Emma the Easter Fairy
- ☐ Cara the Camp Fairy
- ☐ Destiny the Rock Star Fairy
- ☐ Belle the Birthday Fairy
- ☐ Olympia the Games Fairy
- ☐ Selena the Sleepover Fairy
- ☐ Cheryl the Christmas Tree Fairy
- ☐ Florence the Friendship Fairy
- ☐ Lindsay the Luck Fairy
- ☐ Brianna the Tooth Fairy
- ☐ Autumn the Falling Leaves Fairy
- ☐ Keira the Movie Star Fairy
- ☐ Addison the April Fool's Day Fairy
- ☐ Bailey the Babysitter Fairy

■ SCHOLASTIC

Find all of your favorite fairy friends at
scholastic.com/rainbowmagic

HIT entertainment

RMSPECIAL13

The Rescue Princesses

These are no ordinary princesses—
they're Rescue Princesses!